ATLANTIC OCEAN

'MTER

N

W

E

S

LAND LIGHTHOUSE

 THE WRECK OF THE WILLIAM LEE

LEGACY PUBLICATIONS

HERMY THE HERMIT CRAB GOES SHOPPING

BY ANDREA WEATHERS / ILLUSTRATION BY BOB THAMES

HERMY THE HERMIT CRAB lived on the bottom of the sandy floor of the Atlantic Ocean with all of his family and friends. They lived southwest of the barrier island called Folly–just off the coast of Charleston, South Carolina.

IT WAS A BEAUTIFUL PLACE to live. All around were clusters of Seaweed swaying with the ocean currents. There were brightly colored Corals in purple, red, yellow, orange, and white.

Schools of Spadefish with glistening stripes of silver and black swam nearby.

Here, hundreds of Hermit Crabs made their homes in many different kinds of shells.

Some, called Periwinkles, were round and smooth. Others, called Whelks, were long with ridges.

There were tiny Hermit Crabs with tiny Tulip Shell homes, and there were large Hermit Crabs with large Snail Shell homes.

HERMY LIKED HIS SHELL. It was a round Atlantic Moon Snail Shell—marked with colored bands of blue and brown. But the Moon Shell was getting too tight for him. He could hardly climb inside at night when it was time for bed, and his long legs stuck out too far.

When Hermy was walking really fast, he could barely hold on to his shell.

One day Hermy decided it was time to shop for a new shell. He said goodbye to his family and friends and set off on his journey.

Traveling northwest, Hermy came to a Salt Marsh on the Folly River filled with tall Marsh Grass. He almost ran into a Huge Horseshoe Crab crawling slowly in the shallow pools of water. But there was no shell here for Hermy the Hermit Crab.

HE WATCHED A FINE FIDDLER CRAB digging pluff mud out of his home.

But there was no shell here for Hermy the Hermit Crab.

WITH THE OUTGOING TIDE, Hermy was carried around the southern point
of the narrow island of Folly. Soon he was adrift underneath the Folly Beach Fishing Pier.
A Bright Blue Crab was scavenging for food around the barnacle-covered pilings.
But there was no shell here for Hermy the Hermit Crab.

CONTINUING HIS SEARCH, Hermy rode the incoming waves to shore. He could see the Morris Island Lighthouse in the distance from this lovely section of deserted beach.

A Shy Sand Dollar was burying itself in the soft mud. But there was no shell here for Hermy the Hermit Crab.

HEADING NORTHEAST across Lighthouse Inlet, Hermy arrived at the base of the towering lighthouse. He spotted a Wise Whelk shading itself among the faded bricks in the shallow water. But there was no shell here for Hermy the Hermit Crab.

AS HERMY MADE HIS WAY through the powerful waves into deeper water, a Swift

Sea Horse came swimming along. But there was no shell here for Hermy the Hermit Crab.

THE STRONG CURRENTS pulled Hermy north into the Charleston Harbor. Floating past the old foundation of Fort Sumter, he spied a Spiny Starfish clinging gracefully to the underside of a huge rock. But there was no shell here for Hermy the Hermit Crab.

ON A NORTHWEST COURSE to the peninsula of Charleston, Hermy arrived downtown near the Rainbow Row of historic homes. A Proud Pelican was enjoying a fine catch of fresh fish. But there was no shell here for Hermy the Hermit Crab.

BY NOW IT WAS GETTING DARK and was almost time for bed. Turning south, Hermy marched back out to sea. Searching for a safe place to spend the night, he came upon the ancient shipwreck of the *William Lee*.

As Hermy peeked into an opening hidden in the shadows of the old, sunken whaling ship, he noticed a shell shining in the silvery light from the moon. It did not move, so Hermy wasn't scared. As he scurried forward, Hermy spotted the familiar black and brown swirls resembling a shark's eye. Why, it was an empty Moon Shell! Yes, there was a shell here for Hermy the Hermit Crab!

Hermy closely inspected the abandoned Snail Shell. The size appeared to be just slightly larger than his own shell. He turned it over several times to make sure it was in perfect condition. Hermy also measured the inside of the shell with his front legs.

Quickly, Hermy climbed out of his old, tight, little shell and tried on the new Moon Shell. It was a perfect fit and had plenty of room for him to grow! His legs did not hang out of the larger shell, and it felt very smooth inside. He twisted his soft body around the center column of the shell, and curled up for a good night's sleep.

THE NEXT MORNING, HERMY was awakened by a friendly school of Mud Minnows who were darting around him. He was anxious to go home and show his new treasure to his family and friends. But Hermy also wanted to show his new shell to the friends he had met on his shopping trip. In exchange for his new shell, Hermy left his old shell behind at the shipwreck, and he began the long trip home.

At her nesting ground on Shute's Folly, the Proud Pelican was very impressed with Hermy's new shell.

AT FORT SUMTER, the Spiny Starfish smiled at Hermy when he passed by.

THE SWIFT SEA HORSE raced around in a circle to admire Hermy's new shell.

STILL NESTLED among the bricks, the Wise Whelk nodded approval when Hermy strutted by the lighthouse.

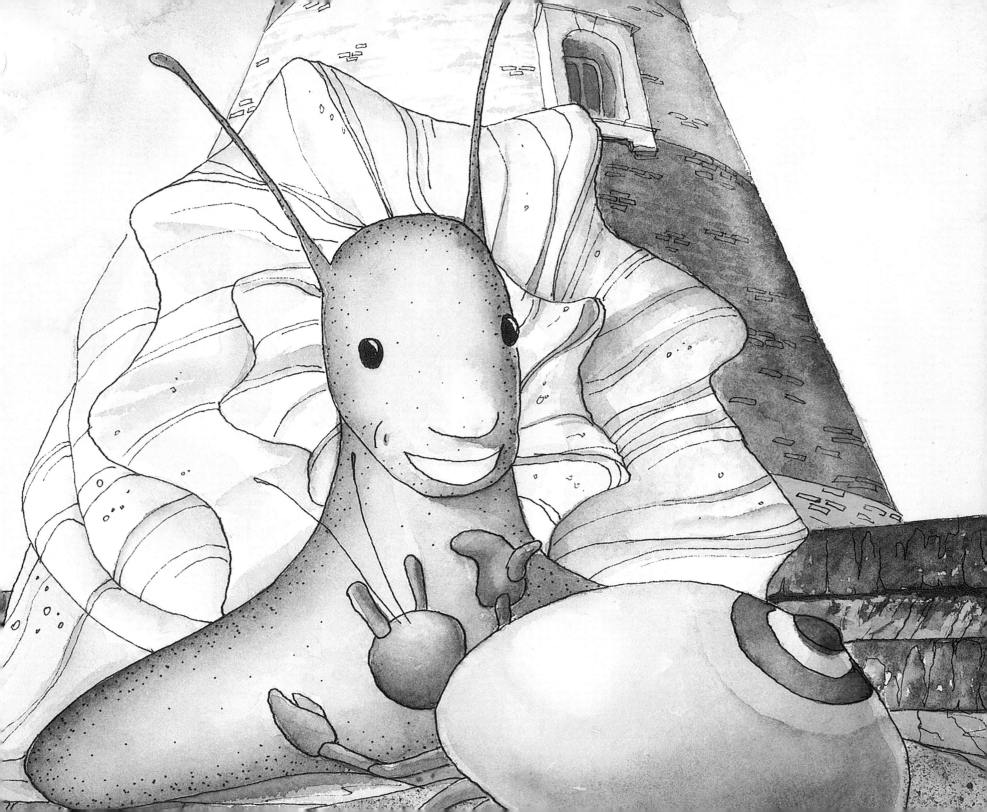

THE SHY SAND DOLLAR peeked out of the mud and winked at Hermy when he stopped to rest on the beach.

AT THE FISHING PIER, the Bright Blue Crab waved at Hermy as he drifted along with the currents.

FROM HIS HOME in the marsh, the Fine Fiddler Crab saluted Hermy with his larger claw.

IN THE TIDAL POOL, the Huge Horseshoe Crab swished its tail at Hermy as he hurried through the shallow water.

At last Hermy was home. All of his family and friends gathered around to check out his new shell. They loved his new house and were glad he was back. Hermy the Hermit Crab was happy to be home, too. What a successful shopping trip!

HERMY'S BEACHSIDE GLOSSARY

ATLANTIC OCEAN / The large body of salt water touching the eastern shore of the United States.

ATLANTIC MOON SNAIL SHELL / A smooth single-spiral shell, tan with bands of blue-gray to brown, common on South Carolina beaches. The darker center and round shape give it the appearance of an eyeball—hence, the nickname "Shark Eye." It can be 1/4 inch to 5 inches in diameter.

BARRIER ISLAND / An island running parallel to the mainland. By taking the full force of storms and hurricanes, a barrier island protects the mainland. There are 35 barrier islands off the coast of South Carolina.

BARNACLE / A type of shellfish that attaches itself to rocks, pilings, boats, and shells.

BLUE CRAB / The bright blue, edible swimming crab common along the Atlantic coast of the United States.

CHARLESTON HARBOR / The body of water that lies inland from the Atlantic Ocean, formed by the Ashley and Cooper rivers, bordering the peninsula of Charleston. All large ships that enter the seaport go through the channel in this harbor.

CHARLESTON, SOUTH CAROLINA / One of the oldest cities in the United States, settled in 1670. Charleston is a seaport situated on a small peninsula laced with marshes and beautiful beaches. This charming city offers locals and tourists many historical sites reflecting its magnificent architecture in churches, homes, gardens, plantations, forts, monuments, and shops.

CORAL / A colony of tiny sea animals that grow in the shape of a bush with many branches. The coral that washes up on Charleston area beaches is called Sea Whip Coral, formed in colors of yellow, orange, red-burgundy, and white.

FIDDLER CRAB / Named for the appearance of the male crab, who has one oversized claw that he waves back and forth as if imitating the movements of a fiddle player. Large groups of Fiddler Crabs make their homes by digging holes in the mud of salt marshes and tidal flats.

FOLLY BEACH, SOUTH CAROLINA / The city, located only 20 minutes south of Charleston, is a favorite family vacation destination.

FOLLY BEACH FISHING PIER / The popular Edwin S. Taylor Fishing Pier is 25 feet wide and extends more than 1,045 feet into the Atlantic Ocean from Folly Beach.

FOLLY ISLAND / The barrier island that lies about 6 miles south of Charleston. The word "Folly" is Old English, meaning "an area of dense foliage." According to historic maps, many other small barrier islands were also called "follies."

FOLLY RIVER / The body of water separating Folly Island from other barrier islands and the mainland.

FORT SUMTER NATIONAL MONUMENT / The fort located at the entrance to Charleston's harbor where the first shots of the Civil War were fired. Built on a sandbar with granite rocks from Maine, the fortification was constructed beginning in 1828 for the purpose of protecting the eastern seaboard from the British.

HERMIT CRAB / A common crab in the shallow waters of the Carolinas. A hermit crab's natural shell is shed through a process called molting when the shell is outgrown. The back of its body is soft and needs protection from its predators; therefore it must seek a shell discarded by another animal such as a snail. When it outgrows the adopted shell, it must find a larger one.

HISTORIC / Something that has its base in the past. Many Charleston homes and buildings are considered historic because they were built in the 1700s and 1800s and are worth preserving for future generations.

HORSESHOE CRAB / One of the oldest known living species of animals, having a pointed tail and a body shaped like a flattened helmet. The animal uses its long, pointed tail to right itself when it is flipped upside down.

LIGHTHOUSE INLET / The body of water lying between Folly Island and Morris Island where the Morris Island Lighthouse stands. The old lighthouse was built on Morris Island, but the rising Atlantic Ocean has covered the southern portion of the island, leaving the lighthouse surrounded by water most of the time.

MARSH GRASS / Tall blades of grass that thrive in the salt marsh, providing food and shelter for many marine animals, including shrimp, fish, and crabs. Spartina is the most common species of grass in South Carolina marshes.

MOON SNAIL / A mollusk with a smooth single spiral shell.

MORRIS ISLAND LIGHTHOUSE / An abandoned lighthouse built in 1876, standing 155 feet high and featuring painted bands–three white and two black–that are fading to the original red brick color.

MUD MINNOW / A very small fish commonly used as bait.

OCEAN CURRENT / The strong flow of ocean water in a definite direction.

PELICAN / The brown pelican is a huge bird commonly observed in coastal areas. It can be seen in flight, nesting on the ground on barrier islands, or perched on pilings or sandbars. It weighs only about 8 pounds but has a wingspan of up to 6 or 7 feet.

PENINSULA / A body of land that is almost completely surrounded by water. The Charleston peninsula is a good example.

PERIWINKLE SHELL / A small, gray spiral shell that once housed a living Marsh Periwinkle Snail.

PILINGS / The upright, tall poles made of wood or concrete that support a structure such as a dock or fishing pier above the water.

PLUFF (OR PLOUGH) MUD / The thick, mucky mixture of mud, sand, and clay observed at low tide in the coastal marshes and tidal flats.

RAINBOW ROW / A row of three-story houses painted different colors on East Bay Street in Charleston. Originally built individually in the 1700s, they once housed shops on the street level while the owners lived upstairs. The different colors were introduced in the 1930s during the preservation effort. This is one of the most photographed areas in all of Charleston.

SALT MARSH / Where the land meets the sea, providing a grassy habitat for plants and animals. A salt marsh serves four purposes: 1) It serves as a nursery for young animals that are born and kept there. 2) It is a sponge that absorbs water and helps prevent flooding. 3) It is a "refrigerator" providing food for the animals. 4) It filters out water pollution. A marsh is exposed and dry at low tide (with a very strong smell) and is partially covered with salt water at high tide. The area where fresh river water drains into salty sea water is called an estuary. In South Carolina, an estuary is a salt marsh ecosystem–one of the most productive areas on Earth, along with the coral reef and the rain forest.

SAND DOLLAR / This sea animal has a thin circular body about 2 to 4 inches wide. Sand dollars live in clusters on the bottom of the ocean, lying parallel to the shore. Their white skeletons can be found at low tide in ankle-deep water and on the sandbars between a gully and the shoreline. A living sand dollar is covered with brown to dark green short, furry spines to burrow into the mud.

SEA HORSE / A small fish with a head that looks like a horse's and a long curling tail that it uses to wrap around objects.

SEAWEED / A marine plant with leaves, rubbery to the touch.

SHARK EYE / Another name for the Atlantic Moon Snail Shell. The center of the spiral is dark brown and black, resembling the eye of a shark.

SHIPWRECK / The remains of a wrecked ship. On December 18, 1861, the first 16 "stone fleet" vessels, filled with granite, were purposely sunk in a checkerboard pattern off the coast of Charleston to block the entrance to Charleston Harbor against Union ships during the Civil War.

SHUTE'S FOLLY / A small island in Charleston Harbor that provides a nesting ground for pelicans and other shorebirds. It is still home to one of Charleston Harbor's earliest fortifications–Castle Pinckney.

SPADEFISH / A disc-shaped fish with sharp-spined fins, found in the waters off the south Atlantic coast. It resembles the Angelfish with its bold stripes of silver and black.

STARFISH / This sea animal has five spiny arms that can grow back if broken off. Starfish live buried in the mud and cling to the underside of rocks, where they can be found at low tide.

TIDAL POOL / A shallow pool of water left behind by the ocean at low tide.

TULIP SHELL / There are two kinds in the Carolinas. The common Banded Tulip has seven distinct brown lines around it and reaches 4 1/2 inches in length. The less common True Tulip has 15 circling lines and reaches 9 to 10 inches in length.

WHELK / A very large marine snail with a spiral shell. The Knobbed Whelk is the most common whelk shell on Charleston's coast, with knobs along its spiral lines and its opening on the right. The inside opening is orange and white. The outside displays vertical lines of purple to brown.

"WILLIAM LEE" / An old whaling ship, weighing 311 tons, purposely sunk in 1861 about 4 miles off the coast of Charleston.

THE HERMIT CRAB is an amazing creature that entertains and amuses many seaside visitors. Hermit crabs are common in the shallow tidal pools left on the beach by the receding tide or in the mud flats of a marsh. They also live in deepwater marine habitats, as well as coral reefs.

The two most common local hermit crabs are the Long-clawed Hermit Crab, *Pagurus longicarpus*, and the Flat-clawed Hermit Crab, *Pagurus pollicaris*.

Men were called hermits when they went into seclusion in order to pray and commune with God. But hermit crabs are not the lone characters that their name suggests. Quite the opposite is true. Hermit crabs live together in colonies, which sometimes support hundreds of hermit crabs. The name comes from the crab's habit of retreating inside its shell when approached by a predator or by a beachcomber.

The shell of a hermit crab is very important. It protects the animal from predators and prevents the soft body from drying out. The crab's soft abdomen twists to the right to wrap around the central column of the shell of a dead snail. If a shell is too tight, it will prevent the animal from being able to reproduce. Hermit crab populations are limited by the abundance of shells. The hermit crab and its shell also provide a home for a variety of other marine animals, such as sea anemones, worms, and tiny porcelain crabs. Hermit crabs should never be pulled out of their shells.

Hermit crabs eat both animal and vegetable matter. They feed on detritus, algae, and live animals, and scavenge dead ones. As the hermit crab grows, it molts, or sheds its upper body shell to make room for growth. It also must find a larger abandoned snail shell. A hermit crab will spend a great deal of time searching for and selecting a new shell, and is very picky when it comes to shell "buying." Hermit crabs will consistently pick one particular species of shell over another. The hermit crab will turn the prospective shell over several times to inspect the outside. Then it will climb out of its old shell and into the new shell so fast that it is easy to miss this exchange. When satisfied with the new shell, the hermit crab will leave the old shell behind and inhabit the new one.

Some hermit crabs have claws of equal size, while others have one claw that is slightly larger than the other one. Most hermit crabs are right-handed, with the right claw being larger than the left.

I dedicate this book to Leslie, Lindsey, and Millie, my three daughters who share my love for the beach. — *AGW*

I dedicate this book to Carol McDaniel and Chevis Clark. Thanks for being my teachers, friends, and mentors. — *RET*

Special thanks to WHIT MCMILLAN, Conservation Education Manager at the South Carolina Aquarium,
formerly with the South Carolina Department of Natural Resources, for his extensive knowledge of sea life.
Special thanks to REBECCA MCSWAIN, our Charleston editor, for her support and encouragement.
Thanks to the fine folks at FIRST BAPTIST CHURCH SCHOOL in downtown Charleston for their support and enthusiasm
for Hermy to become a "real" book!

Text © 2001 Andrea Weathers / Illustration © Bob Thames

THIRD PRINTING 2011

Library of Congress Control Number: 2001132611

ISBN 978-0-933101-20-3

Legacy Publications, 1301 Carolina Street, Greensboro, NC 27401 / www.legacypublications.com
Manufactured by Friesens Corporation in Altona, MB, Canada; March 2011; Job # 63834

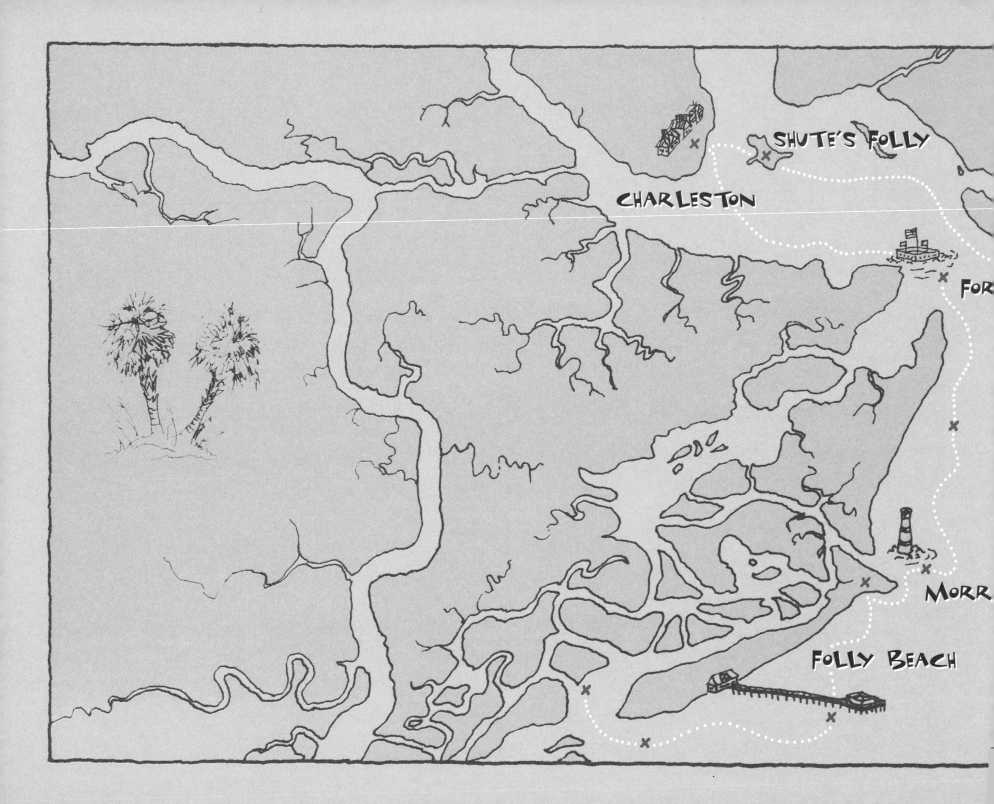